To Miranda and Edwina

Other books about Melric the Magician:

Melric and the Petnapping
Melric and the Sorcerer
Melric the Magician who Lost His Magic

First published in Great Britain in 2015 by Andersen Press Ltd.,
20 Vauxhall Bridge Road, London SW1V 2SA.
Paperback edition first published in 2016.
Copyright © David McKee, 2015.
The rights of David McKee to be identified as the author and illustrator
of this work have been asserted by him in accordance with the
Copyright, Designs and Patents Act, 1988.
All rights reserved.
Colour separated in Switzerland by Photolitho AG, Zürich.
Printed and bound in Malaysia.

10   9   8   7   6   5   4   3   2   1

British Library Cataloguing in Publication Data available.
Hardback ISBN 978 1 78344 162 4 (Second edition)
Paperback ISBN 978 1 78344 210 2

FSC
www.fsc.org

MIX
Paper from
responsible sources
FSC® C012700

EAST RIDING
OF YORKSHIRE COUNCIL

Schools Library Service

FICTION
2016

Melric

AND THE DRAGON

David McKee

ANDERSEN PRESS

Melric, the magician, was watching the king inspect his soldiers. "They are too fat," said the king. "Too much food and too little exercise." It was true. Tummies bulged, faces were smeared with chocolate and swords had been used to make jam sandwiches.

The soldiers had just been dismissed when a messenger arrived.
A dragon had been seen in the east of the kingdom. Soon messengers
arrived from other parts of the country. All brought news of dragons.
"Dragons," said the king. "Just the thing. Tomorrow the soldiers will
dragon hunt. Melric, stay here and amuse my pet troon."

When Melric was alone he thought, "I'd better visit one of these dragons."
He cast a spell, then – WHOOSH – and he was beside a rather young
dragon. The dragon was soon explaining to Melric that he had reached
the age when he had to leave home and find his own place to live.
"I like it here," said the dragon. "But everywhere people run away from me.

You'd think I wanted to eat them."

"What do you eat?" Melric asked.

"Anything really," the dragon sighed. "I love chocolate cake."

Melric laughed, "Just like the soldiers." Then he remembered the dragon hunt.

"The king won't want to hear that there's just one friendly dragon," said Melric, "and the soldiers do need the exercise. I'll ask my sister Mertel to hide you." Melric conjured up some sandwiches for the dragon and then left. Mertel said she was sorry but her cave was too small. Perhaps their cousin Guz the wizard could help?

Guz lived on an island with lots of pets. "They all have chicken pox," he said. "It wouldn't be fair to let the dragon catch it."

Back in his room Melric thought, "Tomorrow nowhere will be safe for the dragon. Kra could help me. He has before, but I don't like to bother him." Suddenly in the smoke of the fire Melric could see Kra. Melric didn't have to bother him, he had come to Melric!

Kra spoke. "Melric, did you hear about the boy who left toys all over his room? His mother said, 'There are toys everywhere.' 'Not everywhere,' said the boy. 'There are none in the toy cupboard.'"

"Thank you Kra," said Melric. The problem was solved.

Melric returned to the dragon and explained his plan. He showed the dragon a hidden entrance to a tunnel and said, "Tomorrow, when you hear the soldiers leaving the castle, go through here."

The next morning the king and the soldiers noisily left the castle. Each group was eager to be the first to find a dragon. Melric waved goodbye and hoped that the dragon would remember what to do.

Bowmen shot the first dragon. Unfortunately it was a boy's kite. They had to pay for a new one. That wasn't the only mistake. The soldiers attacked dragons on carpets, dragon paintings, dragon toys, even a fancy dress dragon.

The Red Dragon Inn sign was attacked. The innkeeper laughed, saying that it made a good story to tell. The smoke was a bonfire, not a fiery dragon, but it was still beaten to death. Everywhere the soldiers were attacking non-dragon dragons.

All day the solders climbed and searched and splashed and squelched
and charged, but not one real dragon was found. As night fell, the king's
bugler called them back to the castle.

The tired soldiers marched home. "Well done, men," said the king. "We've rid the kingdom of dragons!" He was wrong. There, playing with his pet troon, was a dragon. "Meet the troon's new friend," said Melric. "He hid here. It was the only place without toys – I mean soldiers."

"The troon's friend?" said the king. "Well, friend, live here with us."
The dragon was delighted. He now had a home and friends. The king was happy too. "Nobody would attack a king who has a dragon," he thought, "even if his soldiers are a bit fat."
"Was there a reward for finding a dragon?" Melric asked.
"Of course," said the king. "Chocolate cake and plenty of it!"